DATE DUE

JUN 2 1991	JUL 1 1993	JE 01 '1	
JUL -8 1991	AG 30 '0	OC 26 '1	
JUL 15 1991	AN 03 1995	MY 27 '1	
AUG 5 199	CE 21 '95	OC 30 '1	
SEP 23 1991	APR 03 1995		
OCT 21 1991	MY 02 '95		
NOV 19 1991	JE 20 '95		
NOV 30 1991	AG 22 '95		
APR 11 1992	FE 24 '97		
MAY 14 1992	JE 16 '97		
JUN 09 1992	MY 03 '99		
JUN 30 1992	MR 20 '0		
JUL 09 1992	MAR 24 '06		
NO 16 '92	NO 05 '1		
AP 10 '9	FE 01 '12		
MAY 11 '9	FE 25 '12		
JY 30 '9	AG 06 '1		
	AP 08 '1		

GAYLORD · PRINTED IN U.S.A.

WALLY, the Worry-Warthog

WALLY, the Worry-Warthog

by Barbara Shook Hazen
Illustrated by Janet Stevens

Clarion Books · New York

For Brack, for always seeing the bright side.
— B.S.H.

To all my worries.
May they disappear with the mutant mosquitoes!
— J.S.

Watercolors were used to create the full-color artwork.
The text is 14pt. Meridien.

Clarion Books
a Houghton Mifflin Company imprint
215 Park Avenue South, New York, NY 10003
Text copyright © 1990 by Barbara Shook Hazen
Illustrations copyright © 1990 by Janet Stevens

Library of Congress Cataloging-in-Publication Data
Hazen, Barbara Shook.
Wally, the worry– warthog / by Barbara Shook Hazen ; illustrated
by Janet Stevens.
p.   cm.
Summary: Wally, a warthog who worries about everything,
discovers that the terrifying Wilberforce has as many fears as he
does.
ISBN 0-89919-896-1
[1. Warthog—Fiction.   2. Worry—Fiction.   3. Fear—Fiction.]
I. Stevens, Janet, ill.   II. Title.
PZ7.H314975Wa1   1990   88-77662
[E]—dc20   CIP AC
HOR 10 9 8 7 6 5 4 3 2 1

Wally was a warthog who worried
a lot about a lot of things
like grizzly bears,

and ghosts,

and little green men from Mars.

School this way →

Worse, he worried about the saber-toothed trolls who squatted under Suspension Bridge, waiting to slash him to slithers every day on his way to school.

Because of them, Wally always carried
rocks in his pockets and walked very fast.

Worst of all, Wally worried about Wilberforce Warthog, who was huge and hairy and never smiled, and always wore big double-thick gloves.

Wally worried about what he imagined was
under those gloves.

Whenever Wally saw Wilberforce,
he fingered the rocks in his pockets,

and avoided him whenever possible.

One day it wasn't possible. Wally and
Wilberforce were both crossing
Suspension Bridge at the same time.

Wally closed his eyes tight, and walked very fast as he neared the middle.

Oof! He and Wilberforce collided midway.
Each backed off and glared at the other.

"Move!" said Wilberforce, swinging his
huge gloved paws like giant pendulums.
Wally said nothing, but pushed *his* paws
deeper into his rock-bulgy pockets.

"MOVE!" said Wilberforce, stomping his feet
so hard the bridge swayed wildly.
Wally pulled his paws out of his pockets to
hold on, and Wilberforce pulled off his gloves.

Both gasped.

Wilberforce gasped at the sight of the mean-looking rocks that clunked onto the bridge boards.

Wally gasped at the sight of Wilberforce's bare paws.

They weren't huge or horrible. They didn't have needle-sharp nails. They didn't have nails at all. They were, in fact, puny and pink and chewed to the quick.

"What happened to your nails?" Wally asked, eyes wide and staring.

"I b-b-bite my nails," said Wilberforce. "I b-b-bite them because I worry."

"What about?" asked Wally, amazed. He'd thought he was the only one who worried.

"I worry ab-b-bout all sorts of things," said Wilberforce, turning red and looking at the ground. "Things like avalanches and earwigs, and the terrible razor-tailed alligators who live here under Suspension Bridge, waiting to munch me to mincemeat."

"And a-b-b-bout you," Wilberforce said.
"I worry about why you hate me and always avoid me,
which is why I chew my nails and my mother
makes me wear gloves."

"I don't hate you," Wally said, taking a small step closer. "But I worry too, about a lot of things like grizzly bears, and ghosts, and little green men from Mars. And I used to worry about what was under your great big double-thick gloves. Only now that I *know*, I don't."

"Worst of all," Wally went on in a whisper,
"I worry about the terrible saber-toothed trolls
who squat here under Suspension Bridge,
waiting to slash me to slithers.
That's why I carry rocks in my pockets,
to protect myself from the trolls."

"Alligators!" said Wilberforce.
"Trolls!" said Wally.

"I've got an idea," Wally said.
"Let's grab some rocks and take a look,
now that there are two of us.
That way we'll see if they're trolls
or alligators."

So they did.

They looked over one side of Suspension Bridge, and then the other.

To their happy surprise, there weren't any saber-toothed trolls.

Or razor-tailed alligators either.

So they crossed the bridge together, talking about
all the other things they worried about.

"Like vampires, and killer trees, and snakes with
laser eyes," said Wally.

"Like ghouls, and crusher vines, and mutant
mosquitoes," said Wilberforce.

Then they went down to the water, and skipped
the rest of the rocks, which was the beginning of a
fine, close friendship.

As well as worrying less.